ANTA CLAWS
TH POLE
nta Claus
rth Pole
North Pole
rth Pole
St. Nickolas
North Pole
Mr. Santa
Father Chr
North Pole

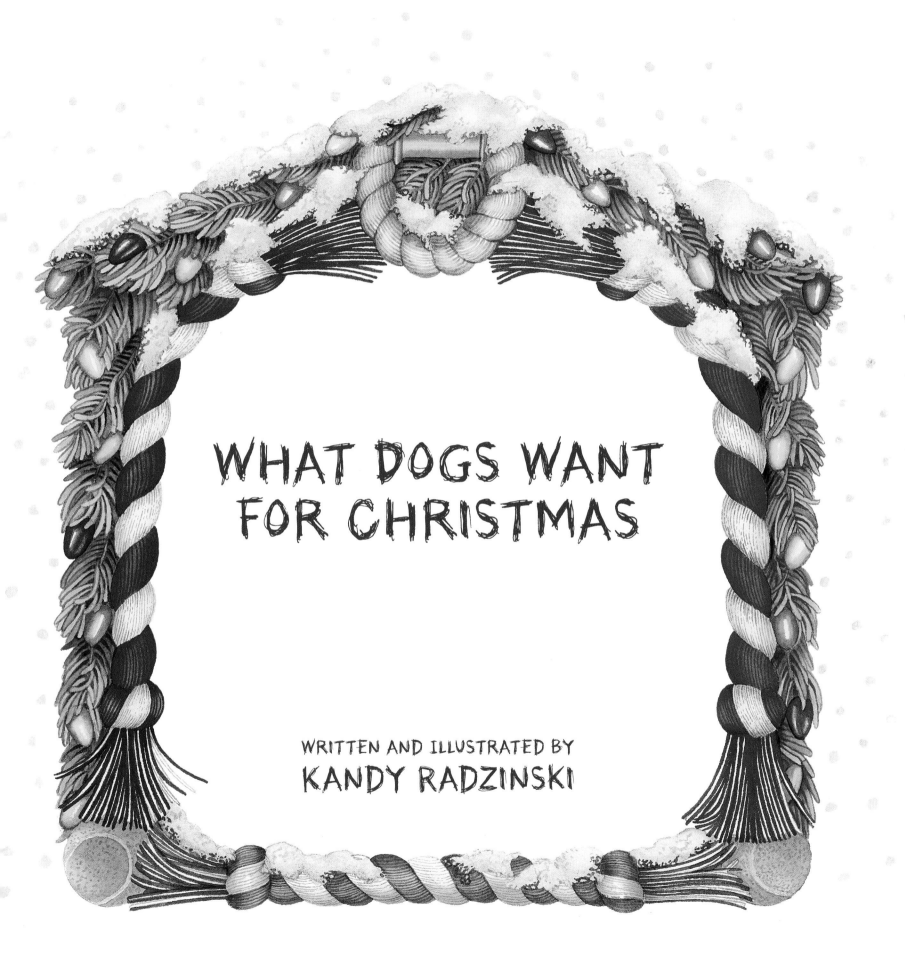

WHAT DOGS WANT
FOR CHRISTMAS

WRITTEN AND ILLUSTRATED BY
KANDY RADZINSKI

Sleeping Bear Press™

310 North Main Street, Suite 300
Chelsea, MI 48118
www.sleepingbearpress.com

© 2008 Sleeping Bear Press is an imprint of Gale, a part of Cengage Learning.

Printed and bound in China.

First Edition

10 9 8 7 6 5 4 3 2 1

Library of Congress Cataloging-in-Publication Data on file.

To Ian on your new journey as you enter college and a new life.
You've blessed me, impressed me and made my heart grow.
Thanks for putting up with me (and my dogs).

Love, Mom

Dear Santa,

I do like eating a nice leather shoe, but maybe I'd better try something new.

Love, Beanie

Dear Santa,

I'd like to help
guide your sleigh.
I even practiced
on my own today.

Love, Harley

Dear Santa,

My ears hang down
to my feet.
Can you fix them
so they're short and neat?

Love, Daisy

Dear Santa,

I know you really, really care.
Please send me something
warm to wear.

Love, Sam

Dear Santa,

I think these treats were meant for you, but it looks like there's enough for two.

Love, Goldie

Dear Santa,

I'd like a frosty new friend
with a magic hat.
Imagine the fun
we could have with that!

Love, Reggie

Dear Santa,
I'd love some mittens made of Persian kittens.
Love, Watson

DEAR SANTA,

I LOVE TO EXPRESS
MY HEART AND SOUL,
SO SEND ME SOMETHING
TO ROCK AND ROLL.

LOVE, BAXTER

KANDY RADZINSKI

Kandy Radzinski received her Master of Science in Art from East Texas State University. She taught art at Central Washington State College and the University of Tulsa. Kandy has illustrated children's books, posters, greeting cards, and even a six-foot penguin. Her books with Sleeping Bear Press include *What Cats Want for Christmas* and *I is for Idea: An Inventions Alphabet*. Kandy lives in Tulsa, Oklahoma with her husband, Mark, their son, Ian, and their dogs, Kirby and Beanie. You can see more of her art at www.kradzinski.com.